A children's picture book about making s<

Written by Caitlin Proctor and illustrated

© 2021 Caitlin Proctor, Deerfield, IL

Printed in the USA

ISBN 9780578997636

Squirrel Soup!

By Caitlin Proctor

Illustrated by Valentina Fedorova

For Michael, Isabel and Colleen. I love you the most. C. P.

For my beloved Mommy. V. F.

It's chilly outside, the winter is coming.

Let's make some soup to warm our tummies.

Grab the ingredients, the pot and the spoon,
we'll mix them all up, it will be ready soon.

We need lentils and ham, salt and black pepper,
add basil and   thyme to make it taste better.

Lentils are healthy and fun to eat!
Add tomatoes for flavor.
Tomatoes are sweet!

Don't forget the veggies!

Carrots, onions and celery.

Add the ham and the broth, now there – almost ready.

A few more things let's read the recipe.

What else do we need?

Bay leaves! That seems silly…

Two garlic cloves, crushed or minced.

Add some oregano, but just a pinch!

Add the water – we almost forgot!

Close the lid. Be careful, it's hot!

Five hours on high to cook the ham soft,

dinner will be ready at six o'clock.

While we wait, let's read a book.

Bubble and boil, the soup will cook.

At six o'clock, let's give it a try. Anything else? Perhaps some salt!
It's time to eat. Serve it with bread and enjoy the feast.

The soup was delicious but look at these dishes!

Shall we tidy up together, in this lovely fall weather?

Wash wash, rinse rinse.

All done. Let's empty the sink.

Let's pack them away, ready for the next day.

Say goodnight to the moon and the stars above.

It's bedtime now, goodnight my love.

A soup recipe to make with your grown-ups!

In a large slow cooker, combine all the ingredients and cook on high for 5 hours. Onions optional!

1.5 c. cooked diced ham

1 c. dry lentils, rinsed

1 c. chopped celery

½ c. chopped carrots

2 garlic cloves minced, or 1 tsp. crushed

15 oz canned crushed tomatoes

½ tsp. each dried basil, thyme and oregano

1 or 2 bay leaves

1 tsp. black pepper & salt to taste

32 oz. chicken broth

1 c. water

CPSIA information can be obtained
at www.ICGtesting.com
Printed in the USA
LVHW070916161121
703386LV00035B/1335

9 780578 997636